Classic Tales

Level 1

The Princess and the Pea

Retold by Sue Arengo
Illustrated by Michelle Lamoreaux

 Contents

The Princess and the Pea   2
Exercises   20
Picture Dictionary   22
About *Classic Tales*   24

OXFORD
UNIVERSITY PRESS

Here is the king. Here is the queen. Here is Prince Harold. And lots and lots of princesses!

'Are they real princesses?' asks
Prince Harold.

'Real?' says the queen.

'Yes, they're real,' says the king.
'Look at them!'

The queen has a book. 'The Book of Princesses'.

'Look! Here's Princess Flora,' says the queen.

'Is she a real princess?' asks Prince Harold.

'Yes, she is,' says the king. 'She's in the book!'

They visit Princess Flora. They have tea with her. But she doesn't talk. She only eats.

'Thank you for the tea,' says Prince Harold. 'We have to go now. Goodbye!'

They visit Princess Val.
They ride with her.
But she doesn't talk.
She only rides!

'Thank you for the ride,' says
Prince Harold. 'We have to go
now. Goodbye!'

They visit Princess Hilda. They listen to music with her. But she doesn't listen. She only sleeps.

'Thank you for the music,' says Prince Harold. 'We have to go now. Goodbye!'

They visit Princess Wendy. They go to her dance. But she doesn't talk or dance. She only sits.

'Thank you for the dance,' says Prince Harold. 'We have to go now. Goodbye!'

They visit lots of princesses.
But Prince Harold isn't happy.

'I only want a real princess,'
he says.

I only want a real princess.

'I only want a real princess,' says
Prince Harold. 'A real … real …
real princess.'

'Let's go home,' says the king.

So they go home.

'Ah! It's good to be home!' says
the king.

'Home, sweet home!' says the queen.

That night there's a storm. The
rain falls. The wind blows.

Then: Bang! Bang! Bang! There's
somebody at the door.

Who is it? It's late! There's a storm!

'Harold!' says the queen. 'Go and open the door, please.'

It's a girl. A beautiful girl.

'It's late,' says Prince Harold. 'What do you want?'

Her hair is wet. Her clothes are wet. Her shoes are wet.

But she smiles at Prince Harold. Her smile is beautiful.

'I want to come in,' she says. 'I am a real princess.'

I am a real princess.

They give the girl new clothes.
They give her new shoes.

'Thank you,' she says. 'What a
night! What a storm!'

'Are you really a real princess?'
asks Prince Harold.

'Yes!' she says. 'I am!'

'A real princess? Let's see!' says the queen.

She takes a pea. A little green pea. She puts it on the bed.

'Bring twenty mattresses!' she says. 'And twenty quilts! Put them on the bed!'

'What a lot of mattresses!' says the real princess. 'What a lot of quilts! What a strange high bed!'

'It's a high, high bed for a real princess!' says the queen. 'Sleep well.'

What a strange high bed!

15

But the real princess does not sleep well.

'There's something in this bed!' she says. 'A stone! A big stone!'

She sits up. She lies down. She sits up again. She cannot sleep at all!

There's something in this bed!

In the morning the real princess says: 'There's something in this bed. A stone, I think! A big stone!'

'Take off the mattresses!' says the queen. 'Take off the quilts!'

Take off the mattresses!

And there is the pea. The little green pea!

'You can feel a pea under twenty mattresses and twenty quilts,' says Prince Harold. 'Then it's true! You really are a real princess! A real … real … real princess!'

You really are a real princess!

'Now at last,' says Prince Harold.
'At last I have my real princess.'

The king and queen are very happy.
Everybody is happy.

And there is the pea! For everybody
to see.

1 Write the words and find the name of somebody in the story.

	1	s	h	o	e	s		
	2							
	3							
4								
	5							
6								

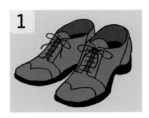
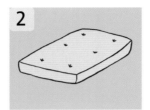

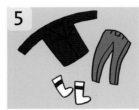

2 Answer the questions. Write *Yes* or *No*.

1 Is the bed high? ____Yes.____

2 Can the real princess sleep?

_____

3 Does the bed have twenty quilts?

_____

4 Is there a stone in the bed?

_____

5 Is there a pea in the bed? _____

6 Is the princess a real princess?

_____

3 Write the words.

dance ~~book~~ pea music tea

1 The queen has a ___book___ of princesses.
2 The king, the queen, and the prince have _____ with Princess Flora.
3 They listen to _____ with Princess Hilda.
4 They go to Princess Wendy's _____ .
5 The queen puts a _____ on the princess's bed.

4 What do they want to do? Join the pictures and words, and write the sentences.

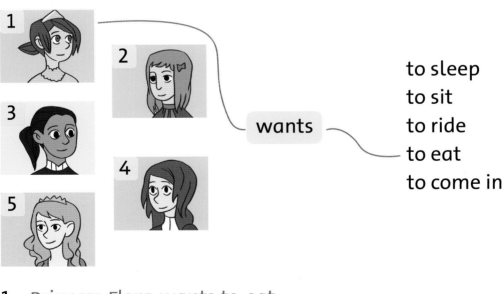

1 _Princess Flora wants to eat._
2 _____
3 _____
4 _The real princess_
5 _____

Picture Dictionary

clothes

king

dance

lie down

hair

mattress

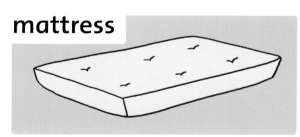

high *The bed is high.*

music

pea